Tales of AKBAR BIRBAL

Published by :
ALKA PUBLICATIONS
2, Sai Sadan, 76/78, Mody Street,
Fort, Mumbai - 400 001. India
Tel. : 2262 4439 / TeleFax : 2263 2585
Website : www.alkapublications.com
E-mail : info@alkapublications.com

An imprint of ALKA Publications

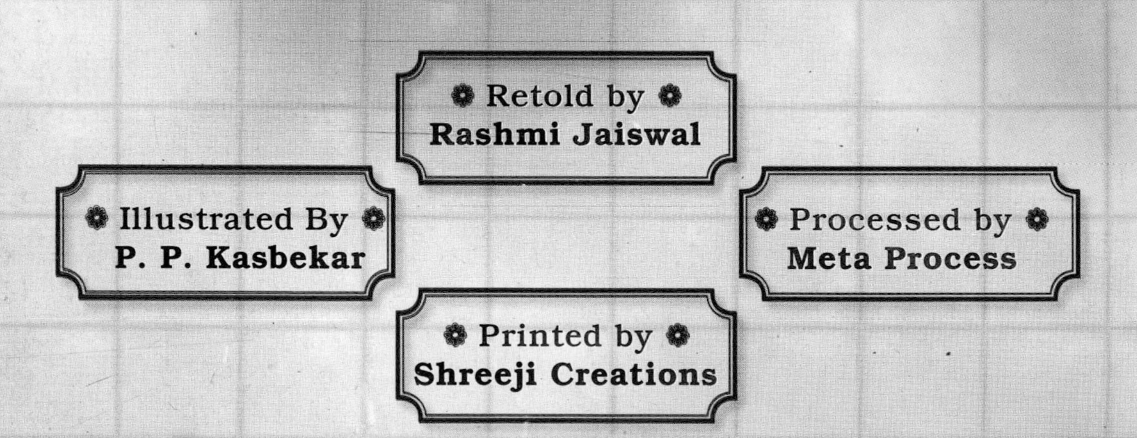

Published by :
ALKA PUBLICATIONS
2, Sai Sadan, 76/78, Mody Street, Fort, Mumbai - 400 001. India
Tel. : 2262 4439 / TeleFax : 2263 2585
Website : www.alkapublications.com
E-mail : info@alkapublications.com

CONTENTS

The Washerman and the Potter

In the city of Agra, there lived a washerman and a potter. Both were neighbours. One day when the washerman was busy in some work, the donkey entered the potter's courtyard. The donkey made his way through the pots and that resulted in breaking of a good numbers of pots.

The potter, when noticed the destruction and

the donkey, he became furious. He picked up a solid strong stick and ran after the beast. The raged potter gave the poor animal a good thrashing. The donkey cried in pain - hee-haw, hee-haw - - -. Hearing the loud scream, the master of the donkey rushed out. "Hey man!" shouted the washerman, "Why are you beating my animal?"

"Oh, so it's yours!" screamed the potter, "This stupid creature has destroyed all my day's labour. Who'll compensate for this, you?"

"Of course, I! Take the money for your broken pots," said the washerman calmly, while paying the compensation.

The commotion had attracted other neighbours too. They witnessed the incident and were very much impressed by the polite and gentle behaviour of the washerman. They were mouth-full of appreciation for the washerman's gentleness.

The potter felt himself been dwarfed by the whole affair. He nurtured a grudge against the washerman and decided to take revenge from him.

After a few days, the potter approached the Emperor, "Your Majesty, I had been to Persia some days back. I felt extremely proud to realise that Persians have great respect for you and have firm believe on your administrative capabilities and justice. But Huzoor! I'm sorry to say - - - ."

The Emperor asked promptly, "Is there something ungraceful? Don't hesitate, speak out!"

The potter replied, "Jahanpanah, Persians do not consider the royal elephants suitable to your grace and honour. They say that the royal elephants look dirty due to their dusky colour. In Persia, the elephants are sparkling white in colour. I came to know that the washerman clean the elephants there."

"O really!" asked the Emperor.

"Yes, Huzoor!" said the potter, "I even know an excellent washerman who will certainly transform the grey elephants into white."

The Emperor at once sent a messenger to call the washerman. When he came, the awkward assignment was bestowed upon him. The washerman was puzzled to get such a task but he dared not refuse and say something in the presence of the Emperor. The potter was rejoiced at his success.

The poor washerman started with the odd job. The whole day, he cleaned the elephants with the best cleansing material, but in vain. At the end of the day, the washerman was visibly tired and was in a miserable state. He sat down holding his head and cursing his poor fate. Just then, Birbal passed from there. He looked at the dejected man and asked the reason for his worry. The poor fellow told him everything. He also apprised him of the evil hand of his vicious neighbour, the potter.

Birbal was a kind-hearted man. He gave a clever idea to the washerman and sent him to the Emperor. The washerman met the Emperor and pleaded, "Jahanpanah, the cleansing process for elephants will take a long time in the absence of a large tub. If you can ask the potter to build a huge tub for the elephants to bathe in the soap solution, then they

would certainly become sparkling white very soon."

Akbar agreed and called the same potter. He ordered him to build a huge pot. After sometime, the potter turned up with the huge earthen pot. The Emperor was happy to see that. "Now the task will certainly become easy," exclaimed the Emperor.

The pot was brought where the elephants were there. It was filled with soap liquid and one of the elephants was persuaded to enter into the tub. The Emperor, Birbal and some other courtiers were also present there to see the strange operation. But to their shock, no sooner did the elephant placed one foot in the tub, it broke into several pieces, as it could not sustain the weight. The Emperor was furious to see this. He roared at the potter, “How fragile have you built the tub! It can’t tolerate even one foot of the elephant. Go and build another pot, but remember it should be strong enough to sustain the weight of the elephants.”

Now the potter was trapped in his own evil net. He fell on the feet of the Emperor and said “Your Majesty even the strongest earthen tub can’t sustain the elephant’s weight. How can I accomplish this job?”

“The same way as you said to clean the elephant to change their colour from grey to white!” shot the Emperor, “I had well understood your vicious will, but I wanted to know why you did so.”

Now the potter confessed his crime and sought pardon. The Emperor said, “I must praise the wisdom of the washerman who forced you to accept your misdeed.”

“No, Jahapanah! It’s not my wisdom but that of honourable Birbalji’s. He gave me this idea to teach the potter a lesson,” the washerman replied.

The Emperor looked at Birbal with pride and admiration and punished the potter for all the inconveniences caused to the washerman.

BIRBAL'S 'KHICHRI'

It was the month of January and Delhi had an extremely cold climate. In a cold morning, Emperor Akbar and Birbal were walking along the river Yamuna. Both were shivering because of the frequent cold waves coming from the river. Akbar bent down and dipped his

fingers into the river water to ascertain the coldness of the water.

"It's terribly cold!" exclaimed the Emperor pulling his fingers out of the water, "No one can tolerate this cold water even for ten minutes."

Birbal disagreed, "I beg your pardon, Your Majesty! A needy man can do anything for money. He can even stand the whole night in this freezing cold water."

Hearing this, the Emperor threw a challenge, "Now you must prove your utterance. I'm ready to give one thousand gold coins to a person who stands the whole night in this cold water". Birbal readily accepted it.

Next day he walked up to the streets of Delhi and located a very-very poor man. This man readily agreed to stand overnight in the cold water for one thousand coins.

Birbal brought the man to the Emperor. Akbar was surprised to know this. He decided to test the man and posted his guards near the river. The poor man stood in the cold water of river without any clothes on his body. After instructing his guards to remain watchful throughout the night, the Emperor returned to his palace. Akbar was almost sure that the man would either not survive from the cold or would escape in the middle.

But to his surprise, the needy man tolerated the freezing cold water the whole night. Next day the poor man was produced before the Emperor.

Akbar asked, "Did you really stand the whole

night in this freezing cold water?"

"Yes, Your Majesty! Whole night I was being watched by your men," replied the man.

"Can you tell me how did you spend the whole night there?" asked the Emperor.

The poor man replied, "Huzoor! I concentrated myself on the street light and spent the night watching the light."

"It means, you got the warmth from the street light. In this case you can not be rewarded. You did not pass the test fully," said the Emperor and sent the man back without any reward.

The helpless man went crying to Birbal and told him about the injustice done to him. Birbal was shocked to hear him. He consoled the man and promised him for the justice.

Next day, Birbal invited the Emperor and a few senior courtiers on dinner. When they all arrived, Birbal welcomed them and took them inside with full honour. The guests chatted for long time. They discussed on different topics. Hours passed this way. But there was no sign of Birbal. He was busy in preparing dinner for the guests.

Unable to tolerate the hunger anymore, Akbar and the other courtiers went to the backyard of the house, where Birbal was cooking the food.

When they all reached there, they saw a strange sight. Three bamboo sticks were tied at one end and the other ends were fixed on the ground. At the upper end, a big pot was hanging at the height of ten feet. On the ground, a small fire was lit.

Surprised by this funny sight, Akbar asked, "What are you doing?"

"Jahanpanah! I'm preparing special 'Khichri' for your dinner," replied Birbal.

The Emperor rebuked, "What a foolish person you are Birbal. How come the heat of this small fire reach up to the pot which is tied up so high?"

"I think it will certainly cook. If the heat from a distant street light can give warmth to a man standing in the cold water, then my 'Khichri' will surely cook,"

said Birbal quite coolly. He again became busy in adding twigs to the fire.

The Emperor realised that he had done a great injustice to the poor man.

He asked Birbal to call the poor man in the court the next day. Hearing this, Birbal served the food, which was already cooked and kept ready. Birbal said sorry for the inconvenience caused.

On the next day, the poor man came to the court and Akbar gave him one thousand gold coins. The obliged man thanked Birbal and went away.

For Few Drops of 'Itra'

It was the occasion of Id and the palace had adorned a new look. Everyone was in the mood of celebration. People were coming to wish the Emperor. The guests were welcomed with the sprinkle of 'Itra' and roses.

Meanwhile, the Emperor was trying to open the bottle of an expensive 'Itra' to apply it on his clothes. Suddenly, the cork of the bottle sprang up and a few drops of the 'Itra' spilled over the carpet. In the spur of moments Akbar at once bent down to save the drops of the spilt 'Itra' and tried to wipe the drops with his fingers. However, before he could wipe, the drops vanished into the thick soft carpet of the hall.

When Akbar stood straight his eyes met with the eyes of Birbal, who was watching him perform the exercise to save a few drops of the 'Itra'. The Emperor felt very much embarrassed.

To save his face, he thought of an idea. Next day, he ordered his servants to empty one of the royal water tanks and asked them to fill the tank with expensive 'Itra'.

Later, he made an announcement that whoever wanted to collect 'Itra' could come and take away, as much as he required.

Akbar's idea behind this announcement was to

show to Birbal that the expensive 'Itra' has no value for him.

The people of the city were very happy to hear this announcement. They praised in volumes for the Emperor's generosity. Soon the Emperor's generosity became the talk of the town.

The courtiers, who were always in search of any such opportunity, came to the Emperor and praised him for his unusual generosity.

Akbar was very happy. However he was unable to relish his fame, as Birbal did not utter a single word of praise for his act of generosity.

One day, when Akbar and Birbal were sitting

together, the Emperor started, "Is it not wonderful to display such an unusual show of generosity? What do you think Birbal?"

Birbal looked straight into the eyes of Akbar and said, "Your Majesty! The loss caused by a few drops can't be made up by spending tank-full of 'Itra'."

Akbar understood the deep root meaning of Birbal's words. The fall from the grace could not be compensated by spending money or by putting any effort.

❀ ❀ ❀

THE 'KHOJAS'

Once due to some reason, Akbar was very angry with the 'Khoja' community and commanded them to leave the kingdom at once.

The Emperor made an announcement that if any 'Khoja' were seen in future he would be hanged to death.

The terrified 'Khojas' were unable to understand where they should go. So they lived incognito for sometime. But they knew that they could not hide for very long. One day, the chief of the 'Khojas' went to meet Birbal and pleaded with him to save them from the Emperor's anger. They told Birbal about their plight and requested him to do something for them.

Birbal was a kind person. He decided to help

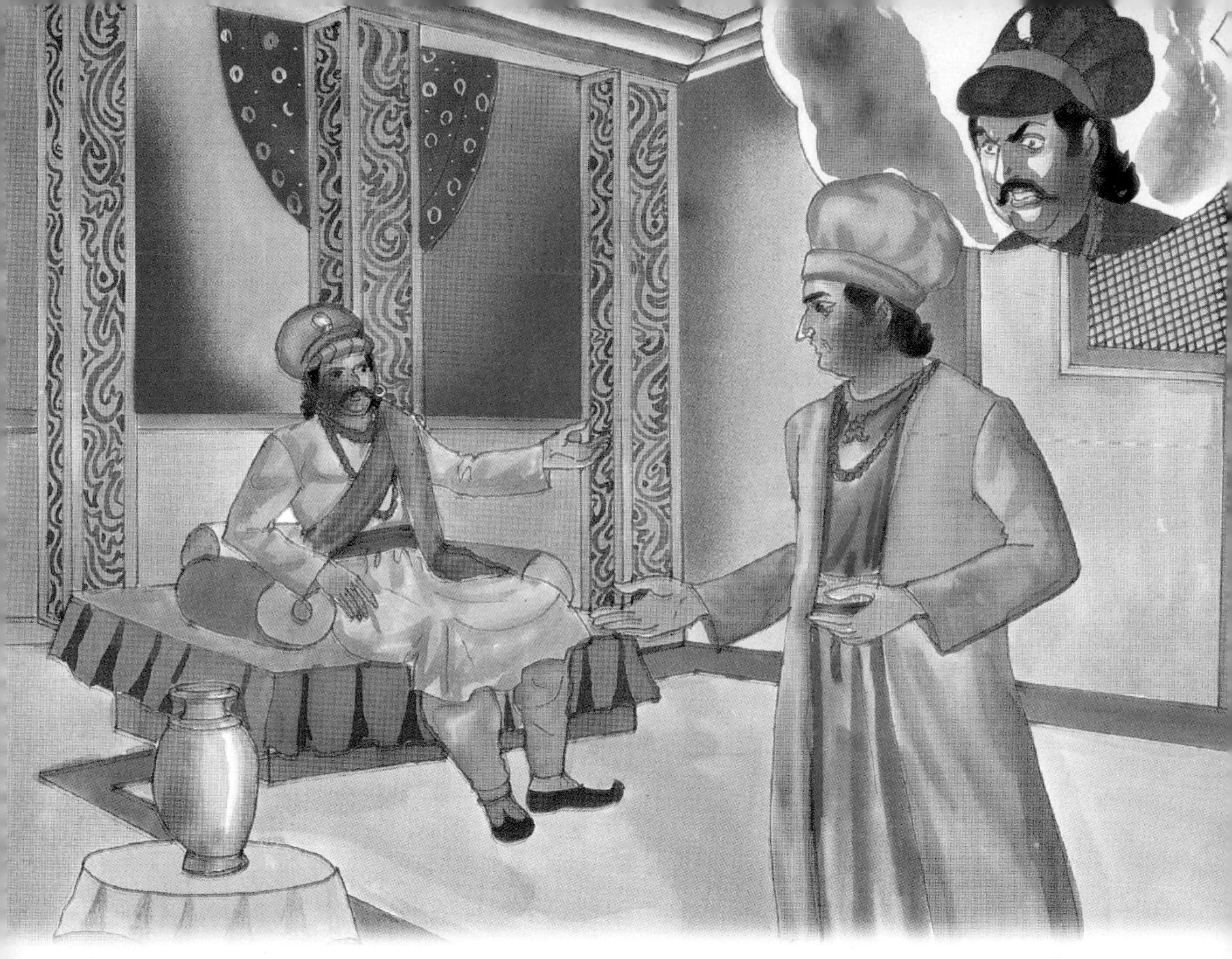

them out from the crisis. He gave a clever idea to the chief as to how to please and pacify the angry Emperor.

Next day, the Emperor went for his routine morning walk. On the way he sighted a strange scene. All the 'Khojas' were sitting on the branches of a big tree.

The Emperor was raged to see the 'Khojas', as they were still in his kingdom. However, he was equally surprised to see them sitting so awkwardly on the various branches of a tree.

Akbar shouted angrily, "What are you doing there on these branches? You are still residing in

my kingdom! This misadventure will lead you to your death!"

The chief of the 'Khojas' replied humbly, "Jahanpanah! It's not our fault that we are here. We tried many times to go away from your kingdom but wherever we went, we found that we were still within your kingdom. As you have instructed us to leave this earth, we are trying to go up in the sky to live there."

The Emperor's anger vanished to hear such a clever and pleasing reply. He forgave them and allowed them to live in his kingdom forever.

The Blinds

One day, Birbal claimed in the court that despite possessing eyes, most of the people of this world were blind.

Birbal's statement appeared very strange to all the courtiers. Even the Emperor mocked at him.

However, Birbal said very coolly, "Your Majesty! At the right time, I will prove what I have said."

After a few days, Birbal went to the heart of the city with the frame of an unwoven wooden cot. There, he placed the cot in the middle of the road and started weaving it. One of Birbal's employees also accompanied him there. As per the direction of Birbal, he stood beside Birbal with a pen and a notebook.

Seeing Birbal doing quite an odd job, a crowd gathered very soon. Each one from the crowd came forward and asked, "What are you doing here?"

Birbal did not answer. He however, asked his employee to note down the names of all the people who were coming and asking him this question. Everybody who approached Birbal, repeated the same question. It went on for hours. The news of Birbal doing an odd job reached the Emperor. Akbar became very curious to know what exactly Birbal was doing. So he at once rushed to see Birbal.

The Emperor reached the place where Birbal was weaving the cot. Akbar was extremely surprised to see Birbal weaving a cot. He immediately asked, "Birbal! What are you doing on this road?"

Birbal asked his employee, "Write the name of the Emperor on the top of the list".

To know what kind of list the employee was making, the Emperor took the notebook from him. Akbar saw the title on the notebook written as – 'List of Blinds' and the name of the Emperor was written on the top of the list.

Akbar fumed to read this. He shouted, "Birbal,

how dare you to write my name in the list of blinds? Am I blind?"

Birbal replied, "I beg your pardon Huzoor but you are indeed blind! You saw me weaving this cot. Even then you asked me what I was doing. I think that only blind persons ask such questions. One after another, whoever came here, repeated the same question."

Birbal continued, "Your Majesty! Once I told you that in spite of possessing eyes, the people of this world were blind. Today, you yourself have proved that I was right."

The Emperor was speechless. He returned quietly to his palace.

❀ ❀ ❀

THE ACTUAL SLAVE

There was a rich man in the city of Agra. The man had bought a slave to work for him. However one day, the slave stole all the valuables from the house and fled away.

Sometimes after the incident, the rich man went to Delhi on a business tour. On his way, he saw the slave coming from the opposite side. He was wearing good clothes. The slave also saw the rich man. The slave reached so close that it was difficult for him to escape from there.

But before the rich man could react, the slave

held the rich man's hand tightly and said, "You crook! You ran out of my house after stealing the money from there. I won't leave you now."

Startled by his sudden move, the rich man could not react for a few moments. Then he came back to his senses and said, "You wicked slave, you are calling me your servant! When I thrash you from head to toe then you'll understand who is whose slave!"

But, the cunning slave continued to behave as if he was the master and he had caught his fugitive slave.

The quarrel between the two, fetched a large crowd around them. The crowd suggested them to go to Akbar's court for the settlement of their quarrel.

So both of them approached the court. Birbal listened to them. The slave remained adamant on his lies before Birbal too.

Seeing the confusing state of affairs, Birbal called his guard and asked him to stand there with a sword in his hand.

Birbal continued discussing the case further. Suddenly he asked his guard, "Cut off the head of the slave!"

The guard sprang up with his sword. The actual slave between the two men was gripped by the situation. He forgot his lies and bent down to save himself.

Birbal's purpose was served. He recognized the slave and ordered him to go with his master and work for him.

THE QUESTIONS

Since long, a few important questions were trickling in the mind of the Emperor. So one day, the Emperor called Birbal and asked, "Birbal tell me, who does go to the heaven and who does go to the hell?"

Birbal replied, "A person who sacrifices his own needs for other's well being, wins the heaven. A person who is self-centered and is ready to subscribe to all the wrong means to succeed in this world, attains the hell.

The Emperor asked, “In this world, what does always grow?”

Birbal said, “It’s the interest of a moneylender.”

“Whom do we call wise and whom do we consider fool?” asked Akbar.

“We call the person wise whose suggestions are useful to us and a person whose help puts us in trouble is considered a fool,” replied Birbal.

Akbar was satisfied to hear the answers given by Birbal. The Emperor said, "Birbal, one last question. Tell me which one is the best season of all the seasons?"

Birbal smiled and replied, "Your Majesty, all the seasons of this world are good so far we have enough to eat and we are happy and comfortable. Else we can't enjoy the prettiest of the seasons."

❀ ❀ ❀

The Most Difficult Task

One day, the Emperor asked in the court, "What is the most difficult task?"

Some said that to fight in a battle was the most difficult task. A few said that labour's job was the most difficult task. According to others, the peasant's task was the most difficult.

However, Birbal had a different answer. He said, "Your Majesty, to pacify a crying child and explain something to him is the most difficult task of this world."

The courtiers in the court laughed at Birbal's answer. Akbar was not at all convinced with Birbal. He said, "You are talking foolish. According to me, pacifying a child is the easiest job in the world."

But Birbal was adamant. "I can prove it," said Birbal.

"Alright! If you prove it, I'll agree to you," said the Emperor.

Birbal said, "Your Majesty, we'll have to play a game to prove it. In this, I'll act as a child and you shall be the pacifier."

The Emperor agreed. At once Birbal got up from his seat and began running in the court hall like a child. He giggled, mischievously pulled a courtier's 'Pagdi', teased someone and tricked others. Suddenly he started crying at the top of his voice.

The Emperor went near Birbal, held his hand and made him sit near his throne. But Birbal, who

was pretending as a child was still crying.

Akbar tried to cajole him but he started crying louder. Then the Emperor called his servant and asked him to bring sweets for the child. The sweets were brought. The Emperor lovingly offered it to the child. But instead of being pleased, he threw it on the floor.

Akbar's temper went up to see his behaviour. However he managed to control himself. The Emperor asked softly, "If you don't like sweets then tell me, what else do you want?"

The child did not answer anything and kept

crying loudly. The continuous crying sounded quite irritating. However, what the Emperor could do now.

He requested the child, "Please don't cry! Tell me how can I make you happy?"

After much persuasion, the child said, "I want to eat sugarcane".

"That's all you want! Why didn't you tell me earlier?" said the visibly relieved Emperor.

He at once called a servant and asked him to bring a bundle of sugarcane. When the sugarcane was brought, the child said, "I want it in small pieces".

The Emperor ordered his servant to chop the sugarcane. But the child began crying again. "I want to eat the sugarcane chopped by you," said the child, who was still crying.

Though the Emperor was quite tired of the child's tantrums, he was not ready to accept his defeat.

So, the Emperor himself took the chopper and cut sugarcane into small pieces. He then placed it in front of child Birbal.

"Now eat it!" said Akbar with a tinge of bitterness in his voice.

Birbal looked at the pieces and began crying again.

"Now what's the problem?" asked Akbar, who looked irritated.

"I don't want these small pieces. I want to eat a long sugarcane," said the crying child.

Almost stamping his feet, the Emperor got up and picked up a sugarcane stick from the bundle. He then threw it in front of child Birbal.

"Eat it! And now for the God's sake, stop crying!"

Akbar screamed.

The child pushed the sugarcane aside and said, "No, not this! I want a whole sugarcane out of this chopped pieces."

The Emperor shouted, "You stupid boy! It's not possible!"

"Why it's not possible? I want only this," said the child crying.

Akbar lost his temper and raised his hand to slap child Birbal.

At once Birbal got up and laughed aloud. He then asked, "Your Majesty, wasn't I right, when I said that pacifying a child was the most difficult task?"

The Emperor agreed, "Yes my clever companion! You were absolutely right. It's the world's most difficult task."

THE THREE QUESTIONS

A senior khoja courtier secretly wished to become Akbar's Wazir. However, Birbal's wisdom always narrowed the chances of the other courtiers for the coveted post.

One day, as usual the Emperor praised Birbal in the court. However, on that day the envious courtier could not tolerate the sky-high praise of Birbal.

He said to the Emperor, "Your Majesty, if Birbal is so much intelligent then he must know the answer of a few of my questions. If he satisfies my queries, I will accept him superior to all of us."

The Emperor agreed and asked Birbal to answer the questions put in front of him.

The senior khoja courtier said to Birbal, "Answer the following three questions –

1) What is the exact number of stars in the sky?
2) Determine the centre of the earth.
3) How many men and women are there in the world?"

Everyone including Akbar was eager to know Birbal's answer. Birbal sought the Emperor's permission to go out of the court for an hour. The Emperor permitted him.

After sometime, Birbal came back with a sheep. The sheep's body was covered with thick hair. Birbal said to the Emperor, "Your Majesty, the answer to first question of my fellow courtier lies in this sheep. The number of stars in the sky is exactly same as the number of hair on the body of this sheep. If my colleague has any doubt, he can count himself and ascertain it!"

Birbal then took out a stick, drew few lines on the floor and pitched the stick in the middle of the lines. He said, "Your Majesty, I have found out the answer to the second question. The centre of the earth is here where I've pitched the stick."

Now, it was the time to answer the third question. Birbal said, "Jahanpanah! It's really difficult to count the exact number of the men and the women separately. In this world there is another group besides the men and the women. And this group is of khojas. These people neither fall under the men's category nor do they fall under the women's category and thus create a good amount of confusion. Jahanpanah! I would request you to kill all such persons who are neither man nor woman, to ease out the task of counting."

Everyone in the court laughed aloud to hear Birbal. However, the ambitious khoja quietly sneaked out of the court.

BEGUM TRICKED

The Empress was very fond of her dear brother Suleman Khan. She wanted the prestigious post of Wazir for her brother. However, the Wazir's post was occupied by Birbal. The Empress was well aware that Birbal was a brilliant courtier and was apple of Akbar's eye. Nevertheless, she decided to plead with the Emperor for her brother. In the evening, when Akbar returned to the palace, the Empress said, "Jahanpanah, my brother is an able person. Besides this, he is your relative. He must get prestigious post of Wazir."

The Emperor exclaimed, "Begum, Wazir's post requires extraordinary intelligence and vast administrative experience. Your brother is novice in this field. Besides this there is no negative reason to remove Birbal." The Empress was adamant. She sternly replied, "Jahanpanah, if there is no reason, then get some excuse for his removal. Give him some work which he could not do."

The puzzled Emperor asked, "Cite me some job for him which he probably could not do."

"Hmm! "Begum thought for some time and then said, "Jahanpanah, tomorrow evening while walking in the palace garden, you ask Birbal to call me from my palace. He will never succeed in his task. And then there will be at least one reason for his removal."

The Emperor agreed. The Empress was very much sure that Birbal would certainly fail this time, as he could not force her to appear in the palace garden.

On the next day when Akbar was strolling in the garden, Birbal accompanied him as per the practice. The Emperor pretended to be disturbed. Birbal asked Akbar the reason for his worry. Akbar said, "Birbal, the Empress is displeased with me and refuses to talk. You know how much I love her. Do something and bring her here."

Birbal agreed and left from there. He at once approached Begum in the palace. Begum was waiting for his arrival. Birbal said, "Begum Sahiba, the Emperor is in the palace garden. He wants you there - - !" Hardly had he completed his sentence a messenger entered the chamber and whispered something in the ear of Birbal. A few whispering words fell in the ears of Begum, " - - - very beautiful - - - No - - no! No need to come - - !" The messenger then left. The Birbal then turned towards Begum and said, "Begum Sahiba, sorry for the trouble. Now you no more required there."

Birbal was gone but the whispering sound was still resounding in the ear of Begum. "About whom the messenger was saying - -, it seems she is a beautiful maiden - - but what she is doing in the garden? It seems because of her the Emperor stopped me from coming there - - - !" thought the Empress who was

badly disturbed and suspicious. She kept on thinking for long time. At last unable to bear her distress and envy, she rushed towards the garden. When she reached there, she found Akbar walking alone. Seeing her there, the Emperor asked, "Begum, you had vowed to force Birbal fail this time. But it seems the whole thing turned in the favour of Birbal."

The Empress was ashamed, "I have been fooled by Birbal. Once again Birbal succeeded. However, I accept his wisdom and take back my words. I will never pressurize you to remove Birbal from his post as he is the most suitable person for it."

The Emperor smiled pleasantly and praised for Birbal in his heart.

CURRY AND THE COURTIERS

One day Akbar and Birbal were sitting leisurely. Suddenly Akbar remembered that Birbal had been to a marriage reception of one of his relatives. So he asked, "Birbal, what did you eat there?"

Birbal said, "Jahanpanah, the feast was fabulous.

There were a variety of dishes." Very curiously, Akbar asked, "What were those?"

"All popular sweets like Laddu, Kalakand, Sohan-Halwa - - - - ," replied Birbal.

"And?" asked, even more curious Akbar.

"Huzoor, there were Pulao, Puri, Missi-Roti,- - - - - and so many other items Jahanpanah. Food was really delicious," Birbal spoke.

The Emperor was about to enquire further about the menu, then only his advisor informed that the Emperor's presence was required for some emergency meeting. So the interesting chat remained incomplete.

After ten days, when the court was in full of its strength, Akbar remembered about the incomplete chat. He asked Birbal, "What else was there Birbal?" Without taking anytime, Birbal replied, "And a variety of curries, Jahapanah." The Emperor was so much pleased with his sharpness and presence of mind that he at once removed his pearl necklace and gifted him.

The courtiers, who were unaware of the whole fact were amazed to watch this and of course were very envious. At the end of the day, the jealous courtiers had a meeting. One among them said, "It seems, the Emperor likes curry very much. He presented Birbal a necklace just for taking its name."

Another courtier added, "We must do something similar to get rewards". The third courtier proposed, "Let's prepare different delicious curries and present them to the Emperor. He will surely be delighted and reward us heartily."

They all agreed to this idea. On the next day, a very strange scene was seen in the court. A number of courtiers attended the court, each carrying a big dish of curry. Seeing the conspicuous sight, Akbar asked, "What's the matter? Why have you visited the court with curry dishes?" The courtiers replied in chorus, "Huzoor! We came to know that you like curry very much. So we all have brought delicious curries for you." The Emperor understood every thing. He laughed, "Ha! Ha! Ha! You fools, the reward, which Birbal got was not for taking the curry name but for his sharpness. Now you all must eat these curries at this very moment!"

And, the courtiers were cursing themselves for their stupidity while eating their curries.

❁ ❁ ❁

THE POT OF WISDOM

Once the Empress pressurized the Emperor to appoint her brother, Gulam Sheikh as the 'Wazir'.

Succumbed to her pressure, the Emperor removed Birbal from the 'Wazir's' post and appointed Gulam Sheikh in his place.

The king of Iran always envied the great Emperor Akbar, whose court was studded with wonderful gems. The king of Iran knew it very well that Birbal was unparalleled in his brilliance. When the Iranian

Emperor received the news of Birbal's removal from 'Wazir's post, he at once sent a messenger with a message. The messenger was also carrying a few pots with him.

The messenger came to the court of Akbar and read the message, "I've heard a lot about your wise courtiers. I need few pots of wisdom for my own use. Please send the pots filled with wisdom. In case, it's not there with you then please send the empty pots back to me."

The Emperor assigned the responsibility of solving the puzzle to Gulam Sheikh. Gulam Sheikh was totally perplexed with the message. He spent many sleepless nights but could not understand what he should do?

At last, Gulam Sheikh went to his sister, the Empress and said, "I'm tired of the 'Wazir's responsibility. I don't want this anymore."

Gulam Sheikh accepted in front of his sister that he was unable to solve the puzzle, which was sent by the Iranian Emperor.

The worried Empress asked herself, "What will happen, if the solution is not sent?"

Finally the Empress called Birbal and sought his help.

After listening to the whole episode, Birbal took all the pots in his possession. He then called the royal gardener and asked him to sow few seeds of pumpkin in the garden. When the plants grew and small fruits came on the plants, Birbal gave the pots to the gardener and asked him to place a small fruit in each pot without plucking it from the plant. Birbal instructed the gardener to allow the pumpkin grow inside the pots.

After a few months, the pumpkin grew into full size and ultimately filled the entire space of the empty pots. Birbal then plucked the pumpkins from their plants. He called the royal messenger and asked him

to take back the pots to the Iranian Emperor. He also sent a message with the pots, "As per your wish, we are sending a small amount of wisdom. It's filled in the pots. Please take it out without breaking the pots."

The messenger reached Iran with the pots. He presented the pots to the Emperor and read the message. After listening to the message and looking at the pots, the Emperor murmured, "It seems, Birbal is reappointed as 'Wazir'. It can't be Gulam Sheikh's wisdom."

The messenger returned to the court of Akbar. He narrated the whole episode. When the Empress came to know about it, she at once told the Emperor to reappoint Birbal at 'Wazir's post.

BIRBAL THE WITTY

Pulling Birbal's leg was great fun for Akbar. One day when the court was in its full strength, Akbar said, "Birbal, last night I had a strange dream. Both you and I were floating high up in the sky. Suddenly we began falling down."

Everyone was listening to the Emperor with great

curiosity. Birbal too was very keen to know the event. So he asked, "Then Huzoor!"

"The very next moment I was plunged in a honey filled pit. I tried to look for you and found you dropped in a gutter beside the honey pit," mocked Akbar, "Birbal, you had actually fallen into the dirty gutter!" As soon as the Emperor completed his statement, the whole court burst into laughter and uproar.

But, Birbal was not a person who could be made object of ridicule. He said to the Emperor, "Jahanpanah, strangely enough the same dream I also had last night."

"Really!" exclaimed the Emperor.

"Yes, Huzoor! The only difference was that you

awoke after falling into the honey pit whereas I did not."

The Emperor asked, "Then you must had seen the dream further. What happened then?"

Birbal replied, "Jahanpanah, after falling into the pit and the gutter, we helped each other coming out of the honey and filth marshes."

"Interesting!" wondered the Emperor.

"Huzoor, we were feeling very uncomfortable with the sticky, wet thing all over our body. So to help us clean, we licked each other," completed Birbal. There was no uproar, no laughter in the court, this time. Only suppressed giggles dared to mock the Emperor. So far, the Emperor was concerned he was speechless.

❀ ❀ ❀

A House in the Sky

"I want a house hanging in the sky!" commanded the Emperor to Birbal. It was a new whim of the Emperor. As usual Birbal accepted his order quietly. However, he sought time for a couple of months and two lakh gold coins. The Emperor accepted both his demands.

Birbal came back home and called a bird hunter. He ordered him to bring hundred parrots. When they were brought, Birbal asked his daughter to teach them a few sentences. Under his observation, the parrots were taught to speak, "Bring bricks! Mix sand and

cement! Start work to build a house!"

Meanwhile, two months passed. The Emperor sent a messenger for Birbal. He was very curious to know about the status of the work. Next day early in the morning, Birbal visited the court with all the parrots housed in a big cage. There in a small adjacent room, he set all the parrots free and closed the room.

When the Emperor came in the court and saw Birbal present there, he became very happy. At once he asked, “How is the work going on? Is it complete?”

Birbal replied, “Jahanpanah, today I am here with all the workers who can go to the sky to work there. It was difficult to find them. But now I'm sure, the work will move fast.”

Birbal then requested the Emperor to visit the adjacent room. When Akbar reached near the room, Birbal said, “Huzoor, the workers are inside. You can give them the required instructions.” With this Birbal opened the room and all the hundred parrots darted out with intense ruffle sound of their wings. The sudden ejection and commotion of the birds puzzled the Emperor. The parrots were shouting in their shrill voice, “Bring the bricks! Mix the sand and cement - - - - build the house!” They were approaching the high sky while repeating these sentences.

The Emperor shouted, “Birbal, What's this silly joke?

“These are workers, Huzoor? They are going to build a house in the sky. I think only these birds can build a house hanging in the sky, Isn't it, Jahanpanah?” asked Birbal.

The Emperor was quiet. Perhaps he was reconsidering his own whimsical order and wondering on Birbal's shrewdness.

The Tailor

Once the Empress got a rare silk cloth piece as a gift from her Chinese counterpart.

She called Birbal and expressed her desire to get a beautiful dress stitched from the cloth. The Empress said, "Birbal, I've heard that tailors always steal some cloth from the cloth piece given to them for stitching.

I'm not worried that a part of my cloth piece would be stolen. However, I don't want that anyone other than me should wear the dress made from this cloth. I want you to make some arrangements so that the tailor can not steal from this cloth."

Hearing this, Birbal said, "Begum Sahiba, my experience says that irrespective of whatever you do, the tailor will manage to steal a part of the cloth piece."

The Empress replied, "No, no! I don't believe it. You call the royal tailor here and ask him to stitch my dress in the palace itself. Depute guards around his work place and then see how he manages to steal a cloth piece. I bet, he'll not be able to do it."

Birbal smiled and said, "Begum Sahiba, the tailors are very smart. Whatever you do, they are bound to steal a part of your cloth piece."

The Empress did not agree with him and took it as a challenge. The royal tailor was called and was ordered to work in the palace. He was told not to leave the palace until the work was finished.

The tailor came with all his essentials to stay in the palace premises. His work place was tightly observed by the royal guards. The tailor was not allowed to go out, not even to his house. Like this, ten days passed. The whole day, the tailor would work on the extraordinary dress of the Empress.

One day, tailor's daughter came to see him. She said, "Father, please visit home today. Mother is remembering you a lot." As the girl was not allowed inside, she remained standing out of the guarded room.

The tailor expressed his inability to visit home.

But the daughter remained adamant. She kept insisting her father. Irritated by her repeated insistence, the angry tailor lifted his shoe and flung it towards her. He said, "Silly Girl! So many times, I have told you that I can't come. Why don't you listen?"

Seeing her father so much irritated, the little girl giggled out of amusement. She picked up the shoe, which was flung at her and ran away from there.

Finally, the dress was ready after fifteen days.

The empress was very happy to see it. She gave good reward to the tailor. Before leaving the palace, the tailor was thoroughly checked by the guards.

The Empress was elated that her dress would be rare in the whole kingdom.

One day, the Empress was passing through the market with her royal cavalcade. Suddenly she noticed a woman wearing a blouse, which was made of the cloth similar to her rare dress.

Astonished to see this, the Empress immediately asked her guards to call the woman to her palace. When the woman came, the Empress asked her who she was. After enquiry it was found out that she was the wife of the royal tailor.

The Empress was angry as well as surprised. She called the tailor. The tailor was very much frightened. He went to Birbal and requested him to come along with him. Birbal felt pity and agreed to accompany him.

The Empress was very angry, but Birbal cooled her down. He said, "Begum Sahiba, it's not the fault of this tailor. The tailors are like this only. Please forgive him."

The Empress thought for a while and then said to the tailor, "I'll forgive you if you reveal how did you manage to take the piece of the cloth out from the palace.

The tailor said, "Huzoor, when my daughter came to call me, I pretended to be very angry and threw my shoe towards her. I had stuffed a small piece of cloth in the shoe. Before coming here, I had already

briefed my daughter about it. So, when I flung the shoe towards her, she picked it up and ran away from there. This way, the piece of cloth was brought out of the palace."

The tailor's head bent down. As per her promise, the Empress forgave him and sent him back.

She then turned towards Birbal and said, "Birbal, you were absolutely right. It's impossible to prevent this lot from stealing the cloth."

Birbal smiled and went away from there.

Effort and Destiny

One day when the court was full in its strength, a discussion began. It was on the contribution of a person's luck and his deeds on his life. Almost all agreed that fate was supreme and ultimate. No one could alter the destiny. But, Birbal had some other view. He said, "Something destined can be changed with the courage and effort."

Since his view unmatched the common thinking, the Emperor decided to test him and his view. Everyday

Birbal would go to take bath in the river. The lane by which he had been going to the riverbank was very narrow. On both the sides of the lane, there were low lands. Akbar asked one of his Mahout to lead an elephant on that lane from the opposite side at the time when Birbal was going towards the riverbank. So did the Mahout. When he saw Birbal, he pushed the spear in the elephant's body.

The elephant cried with pain and started running. Birbal, who was coming from the opposite side, saw the elephant approaching him with a terrific speed. For a fraction of time, he was scared and puzzled. But the very next moment, he decided to oppose the impending calamity. He saw a lean, stray dog standing there on the lane. He hastily picked it up and threw it on the neck of the elephant. The dog was angry and confused. He bit the elephant on his neck. The pain bewildered the elephant and he began running in the opposite direction. Meanwhile, Birbal escaped from there and reached the court. When Akbar saw him, he understood that Birbal came out unhurt with his courage. He praised Birbal and expressed his faith on his view.

❀ ❀ ❀

THE BUYER OF THE ELEPHANT

One evening, the Emperor was passing through the market sitting on the royal elephant. Birbal was also with him. Suddenly a loud call came from behind, "Hey, would you sell your elephant?" The insulting call infuriated the Emperor. He turned his head back and looked at the caller. He was a drunkard. His intoxicated voice and uneven movements were the indication of his condition. The Emperor controlled his anger considering his state and moved ahead.

On the next day, he sent his guards to bring the man to the court. The man appeared before the

Emperor. Akbar asked, “Hmm! So you want to buy my elephant. Right!”

The frightened man replied, “Your Majesty, I apologize for my behaviour. Yesterday’s buyer of the elephant has left the city. I was just a middle man on behalf of him.”

The man was standing with folded hands and lowered gaze. The appearance and clever reply vented out the Emperor’s anger.

Akbar asked the man, "It does not seem to be your answer. Tell me, who taught you such clever reply?"

The man said, "Jahanpanah, yesterday when I came out of my intoxication, I realized my grave folly. I at once rushed to Birbalji and begged him to do something to save my life. He instructed me to answer you so cleverly."

The Emperor, who had already forgiven the man, released him and praised Birbal heartily for his cleverness.

THE HUSBANDS

It was the Emperor's usual practice to roam in the capital in disguise to get the first hand information about his subjects. During such tours, Birbal was his favourite companion. Once in one such occasion,

the Emperor heard a shrill commanding voice of a woman "Go and finish this work today! I doubt your worthiness. Hardly you can do any work properly."

It was an angry wife, who was lambasting her husband for some failure in his work and was commanding him. So far as the husband was concerned, he was standing in front of her, speechless and with bowed head.

Witnessing this sight, the Emperor was very much surprised that a strong, tall, hefty man was behaving in such a subdued manner. Akbar asked Birbal, "Isn't it amazing? It seems that this man has some compulsion, or else why should he be so docile and take commands from his wife!"

However, Birbal differed, "Jahanpanah, I don't see anything unusual here. All the husbands are guided by their wives."

The Emperor was not ready to believe it. Finally, the Emperor decided to test it and called a meeting of all the husbands of his city in a big ground. When they gathered, the Emperor announced, "O respectable husbands of my city! Please divide yourselves into two small groups. The husbands who obey their wives and take commands from them should move on the right side and the remaining ones who act as per their own wishes should come on the left side."

Soon a huge wave of husbands was found moving towards the right. The Emperor was quite disappointed to see this. At the end, he found all but one on the right side. Akbar was very much pleased with the person who was on the left side. He at once called the man near him and said, "I want to award you for choosing the left side. I could find at least one person who is not like the rest of them."

Birbal intervened, "Huzoor! Before awarding him, let me ask a question to this man." The Emperor permitted him.

Birbal asked, "Will you please tell me why did you move in the left direction?"

The man promptly replied, "Your Majesty! Before coming here, my wife had briefed me to keep myself away from the crowd. So I chose the side which was not crowded."

"Ha! Ha! Ha!" The whole ground resounded with the loud laugh, cheer and giggle. Now the Emperor had no option but to believe this secret truth.

Distance Between True and False

Once Akbar and Birbal were sitting leisurely. The Emperor suddenly asked, "Birbal, can you measure the distance between true and false?"

At once Birbal replied, "Why not Your Majesty! It's just the width of four fingers."

Surprised by the answer, the Emperor asked, "How is it only four fingers?"

Birbal replied, "Your Majesty, when we see something from our eyes it is certainly true. But when we listen about the same thing through our ears, it is false. So the distance between true and false is of four fingers."

Happy with the clever reply, Akbar gave him a good reward.

The Clever Reply

It was evening time and the court was to be adjourned after the day's work. At this hour, the chief of the guard informed the Emperor that a learned man from a distant place wanted to see the Emperor and Birbal. Akbar had great respect for the learned people and so he did not want to disappoint him. He asked the chief to allow the man in the court.

The learned man appeared in the court and bowed before the Emperor. He then said, "Your Majesty, I've heard a lot about your wisdom and Birbal's wit. I had a long crave to get the taste of Birbal's wit. I want

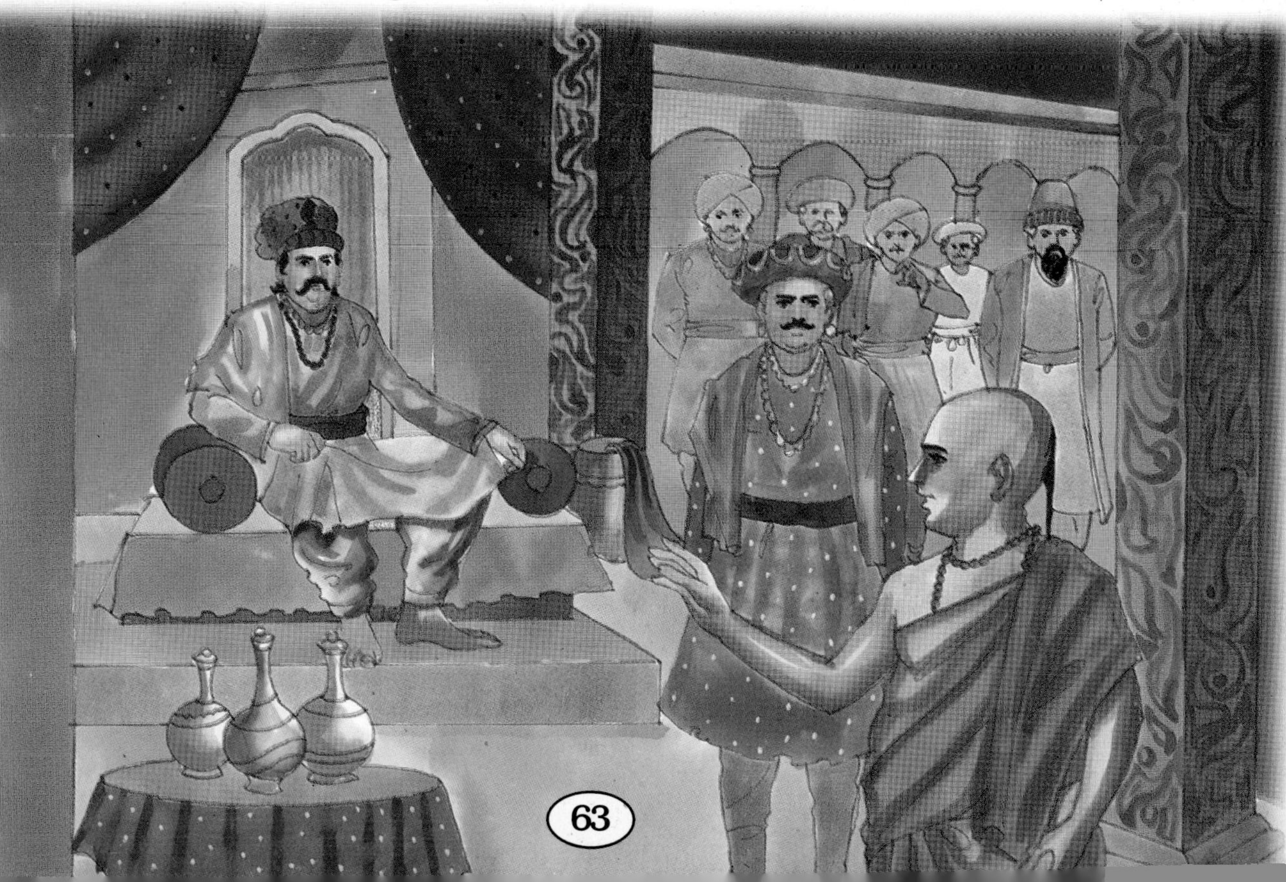

to ask a few questions to Birbalji." Birbal heard him and said, "Yes! What do you want to ask?" The man replied, "Birbalji, I've a set of hundred easy questions. Either you answer these questions or you answer a single difficult question. You can choose any one of these two." Birbal thought, "Hundred questions will certainly take a long time. It would be better if I opt for one difficult question."

So Birbal requested the learned man to ask his single difficult question.

The man asked, "Tell me, which appeared first in this world, a hen or an egg?"

Birbal promptly replied, "Of course hen!"

The man shot back, "How can you be so sure! Is there any proof of it?"

Birbal replied, "If I have not forgotten, you were supposed to ask only one question. Isn't it?"

The man got the taste of Birbal's wit and left the court admiring Birbal in his heart.

THE EXACT PORTRAIT

One day Birbal saw the court's artist quite worried. Birbal personally knew the artist. He was a humble gentleman. Birbal enquired with the artist, "You are looking gloomy. What's the cause?"

The artist said, "Sir, I'm really worried. One big businessman is after ruining my reputation, which I have earned till now."

"What has happened?" enquired Birbal.

"Huzoor, one day I met the businessman in some party. There he was challenging that no artist could portray him perfectly. Hearing this, I accepted his challenge and fixed up the time with him for drawing his portrait. A few days latter when I finished the portrait, I visited the rich man's house and showed the portrait to him. But seeing the portrait, he screamed - You have portrayed me in beard while I don't have any beard! I tried to convince him that at the time of portrait making, he was possessing beard. But he did not listen to me at all."

The artist was in tears. Birbal consoled him and enquired further. The artist said, "Sir, then I humbly

asked him to give me one more chance to prove my deftness. He agreed. After a few days I visited his house with a new portrait. I was quite confident this time. But when I saw him he was a clean shaved man. As I feared, he shouted- 'This can't be my picture. This picture is showing moustache, whereas I don't possess it. I tried to convince him that it was not my fault. However, he declared that I failed to fulfil my challenge. I asked for one more chance but he tricked me the next time too. Only after portraying him for five times, I could understand that his motive was evil and he wanted to let me down.'

The artist then showed Birbal all the five portraits. All the portraits were indeed nice ones. Birbal was a kind-hearted man. He decided to help the artist. He briefed the artist and accompanied him up to the rich man's house. Birbal remained outside the house, whereas the artist entered inside.

As soon as the rich man saw the artist, he said mockingly, "O great artist! You are here again! It seems, you have come again with some of your rubbish item."

The artist humbly replied, "Sir, I'm sure, what I've brought today will surely match with your face."

Saying so, he passed the framed piece to him. The rich man held it in his hand and looked at it. But it was just a mirror.

He screamed angrily, "What a silly joke it is? You've brought just a mirror!"

Then entered Birbal, who was standing outside and was listening to their conversation.

Birbal said, "Are you not happy with the mirror which is showing your exact picture? I think only a mirror can depict your present face. You don't need a portrait but a mirror, my friend."

The rich man was very much ashamed to see and hear Birbal. He begged his pardon for his folly and paid the artist well.

THE LIST OF FOOLS

The Emperor was very fond of tall, handsome and agile horses. Once a merchant from Arabia, came to sell his horses. He displayed a few very impressive horses to the king. The Emperor liked those horses and ordered for a good number of similar horses. He gave

two lakh gold coins as an advance to the merchant.

The man was a fraud. He disappeared with the money and did not return for a long time.

Time passed. One day a unique whim struck Akbar's psyche. He said to Birbal, "I want to see a list of all the fools of my capital. Prepare it immediately!" Birbal affirmed and promised to bring the list after sometime.

After a week, Birbal called on the Emperor with a long list of fools and presented the paper to the Emperor. Akbar was happy that Birbal had accomplished his job in a very little time. However,

when he gazed on the paper, he was raged to read his own name on the top of it. "What's this Birbal?" the Emperor roared, "How dare you put my name in this category?"

"I beg you pardon, Huzoor! You're a justice loving person. Please judge your act regarding giving the advance to a stranger and then tell me, shouldn't I keep you in this list?" asked Birbal with folded hands. The Emperor calmed down little and argued, "Birbal, assume that the man comes with the horses. Then what will you do?"

"I will immediately remove your name and put his name at your place," promptly replied Birbal, the wittiest of all!

THE OWNERS OF THE MANGO TREE

One day, two neighbours Ramlal and Shamlal approached Birbal for the settlement of their feud. The feud was over a mango tree, which was located between their premises. Ramlal and Shamlal were equally vocal about their claim over the tree.

Since both the claimants seemed equally strong with their claims, Birbal found it difficult to settle the matter. So he sought some time to wrap up their dispute and send back Shamlal and Ramlal.

The next day, Birbal sent one of his servants

to the houses of Ramlal and Shamlal with a little briefing. The servant first visited the house of Ramlal. It was evening time. The servant knocked at the door of Ramlal's house. When Ramlal opened the door, the servant said, "Sir, I was passing through the way by your house. I saw a thief who was stealthily plucking the mangoes from the tree adjacent to your house. Being a concerned citizen of the city, I felt it my duty to inform you and so I rushed here."

Ramlal heard him unperturbed. There was no sign of worry on his face. He said to the servant, "Thank you for informing me. But right now I'm busy with some other work. I'll inspect the sight as soon as I get free from here."

Now the servant proceeded towards Shamlal's house. He knocked at the door and when it was opened by Shamlal, he repeated his version to Shamlal. Hardly had the servant completed his statement, Shamlal rushed out towards the mango tree.

Meanwhile, the servant sneaked away and headed straight to Birbal. The servant narrated the whole incident to him.

On the next day, Birbal called both Ramlal and Shamlal. When they appeared in the court, Birbal said, "Both of you appear equally strong claimant of the tree. So I've decided to give one half of the tree to Ramlal and the other half of the tree to Shamlal."

Birbal explained further, "I order that all the fruits of the tree should be plucked and divided between two of you. The tree should also be cut down and the wood should be divided between two of you."

The judgment rejoiced Ramlal. He at once exclaimed, "Your Majesty, I accept your fair judgment and am ready to take my share."

However, Shamlal looked quite aggrieved with the judgment. He pleaded with Birbal, "Your Majesty, I beg for your mercy. Kindly don't cut the tree. This tree is like my child. I've brought it up from the sapling to a fully-grown tree. I can't see its end. I'm ready to give

up my claim. Let the tree be with Ramlal."

Tears rolled down from the eyes of Shamlal. Birbal got up from his seat, consoled Shamlal and said, "Shamlal, your love for the tree proves that you are the rightful owner of the tree." Birbal then turned towards Ramlal and lambasted, "Ramlal, you are a cheat. You tried to grab your neighbour's tree by misleading the court. You must get punishment for your crime."

Birbal then called the guards and sent Ramlal to jail.

The Most Beautiful Child

Akbar loved his grandson Khurram dearly. He was extremely charmed by his innocence and lovely face. He was very much sure in his mind that no other child can be lovelier than his dearest Khurram.

One day, when Akbar was sitting in the court, he shared his view regarding his grandson, "I think Khurram, my dear grandson is the loveliest child in the capital. Isn't it?"

"Indeed Huzoor!" almost all the courtiers affirmed in chorus. However, Birbal chose to remain quiet. "Are you not convinced with my view?" the Emperor asked Birbal.

"No Huzoor! It's not like this. Nevertheless, I think that the perception of beauty varies from person to person," said Birbal.

"I don't agree with you. 'Rose is beautiful' and no one will disagree with this statement. Similarly, no one will differ on 'crow is ugly'. So what is beautiful or what is ugly, people's view will be alike," said the Emperor.

Birbal was not convinced with the Emperor. So Akbar asked him to prove his point. Birbal sought sometime to answer his challenge.

After a few days, Birbal came in the court and said, "Jahanpanah, today I found the most beautiful child in the world and now I want to show it to you."

"Really! Where is it?" asked the Emperor quite surprised, "No Jahanpanah, the child is not here. To see it, you will have to come with me," said Birbal.

The curious Emperor at once agreed to accompany him. A few fellow courtiers also went along. They all disguised themselves so that no one could recognize them. Birbal led them to the outskirts of the city. He further led the Emperor and the fellow courtiers to a narrow lousy place. Everyone was wondering how could Birbal find such a beautiful child here in this filthy part of the city.

At last, Birbal stopped near a small hut. A child was playing in front of the hut. It was a dark complexioned, flat nosed child. Besides this, he was smudged with dirt and mud. Birbal pointed towards the child and said, "Jahanpanah, look at the child. He is the most beautiful child!"

"What?" screamed the Emperor, "Have you gone mad or is this your silly joke? How can you call such an ugly child, 'The most beautiful child'?" Other courtiers too began showing their anguish. But Birbal said calmly, "Wait! You'll soon see the truth in my words."

Suddenly the child slipped on that muddy ground and hurt himself. The next moment the child was crying loudly. Hearing the loud cry of her child, the mother darted out of the hut. She hurriedly picked up the child in her arm and kissed him numerously. The mother was loving her child frantically and was saying,

"O my love, my sweat heart! Please don't cry. O my pleasant moon, O my Angel! I'll punish the ground for its fault." She then battered the ground to persuade her wailing child.

Abhorred with the whole sight, the Emperor who was not standing much far away, said, "What a crazy woman she is? How can she call such an ugly child 'moon'?" The Emperor's words fell into the ears of the young mother. She sprang up and shot bitterly, "Who are you to call my darling 'an ugly child'. Are you blind? Can't you see that he is the most beautiful child of this city? Run away at once from here, else you'll have to bear the brunt of an angry mother."

The Emperor, Birbal and the courtiers at once

moved away from there. On the way Birbal asked, “Jahapanah, wasn’t that child the most beautiful child in the eyes of his mother?” The Emperor who was thoughtful since the incident said, “Birbal this incident taught me that whomsoever we love dearly looks beautiful to us. For a mother, her child is the most beautiful child in the whole world.” Akbar said further, “Birbal I’m thankful to you for opening my eyes for this great, ever lasting truth.”

Birbal was always ready to help the needy. If he was convinced that someone was really good and honest in his work, then he could go to any extent to support the person.

One day, an old man came to him. The man was a diamond crafter. He was excellent in cutting

and polishing diamonds. Once he had a flourishing business. However, when he became old his business was totally marred. He was no longer getting any work.

The old man apprised Birbal of his poor condition and requested him to help.

Birbal assured the old man of his help and gave a big crystal of sugar. Birbal asked the man to cut the crystal at such angles that it would look like a beautiful precious diamond.

Birbal said, "If you are able to do this work dexterously then you can get excellent reward".

After a few days, the old diamond crafter came to Birbal and presented him the sugar crystal. It was now looking like a beautiful diamond. Birbal was very much impressed by his craftsmanship. Birbal took the man to the Emperor.

There, Birbal showed the diamond looking sugar crystal to the Emperor and said, "Your Majesty! This man has brought a wonderful diamond to show to you. Such a big and precious diamond can only be valued by you. So I've brought this man to you."

The Emperor looked at the diamond. It appealed to him. Since the barber was saving his beard, the Emperor kept the sugar diamond in his pocket. After the shaving, the Emperor went to take bath. He, however, forgot to take out the diamond from his pocket. While bathing the sugar crystal got dissolved in the water.

After the bath when Akbar was having his breakfast, suddenly he remembered about the diamond. Akbar ordered his servants to find out the diamond in his clothes and in the bathroom. The

servants searched for a long time but they could not find the diamond.

Next day, the old diamond crafter came to the court to collect the price for his diamond. Since he was already briefed by Birbal to quote a huge sum of money, he asked for fifteen thousand gold coins for the diamond.

The Emperor felt that the price was exorbitant. Nevertheless, the old man insisted that he had put his hard work for long time to cut the diamond so beautifully. The old diamond crafter said, "Your Majesty! My diamond is priceless. However I'm asking only for my hard work. If you feel that the price is high, then please return the diamond to me. I'll go to some other place to sell it off."

What could the Emperor do? There was no diamond to return him. So he called his treasurer and asked him to pay fifteen thousand gold coins to the old diamond crafter.

Later on the old diamond crafter went to Birbal and paid his gratitude.

When Akbar Said No to Birbal

In the court of Akbar, there was a senior courtier named Sultan Khan. He had an unemployed vain young son. The unworthy son was the cause of all worry for his father. One day, Sultan Khan thought of a clever idea to get an employment for his son in the court. He began accompanying his hopeless son to the court. The idea behind this move was to bring his son to the notice of the Emperor. He had planned to request the Emperor at the appropriate time to employ his son in the court.

Though Sultan Khan knew it very well that in the presence of Birbal, it would be very difficult to get an

entry for his unworthy son in the court. Nevertheless, Sultan Khan started bringing his son to the court every day. Birbal noticed the unusual presence of Sultan Khan's son in the court. Sultan Khan's motive could not remain concealed from Birbal's eagle eyes.

As Sultan Khan was apprehensive that his clever move could be turned futile by Birbal, he decided to counter it by poking the Emperor against him.

Very soon, Sultan Khan had a chance to furbish his evil wish. One day, Birbal could not come to the court on time. When Emperor Akbar noticed the absence of Birbal, he inquired about him. Sultan Khan, who was in search of the right opportunity, got up from his seat and replied, "Your Majesty! It seems, Birbal has no respect for the court rules and its timing. Without any prior permission, he is absent from the court."

Akbar knew that it was another desperate attempt to malign Birbal. However, he felt Sultan Khan's words justified.

The Emperor said, "Sultan Khan, you are right. It seems, Birbal has forgotten the rules of the court." Seeing his plan working, Sultan Khan instigated the Emperor, "Your Majesty, you must teach Birbal a lesson." Akbar said, "Sultan Khan! Will you suggest me how can I do it?" The proud Sultan Khan answered happily, "Jahanpanah! Now on, you should refuse all and every demand of Birbal. Snatching away all your favours will certainly bring him to the right senses."

The Emperor thought for a while and then agreed.

After sometime, Birbal appeared in the court. The Emperor asked angrily, "Birbal is this a time to appear in the court?"

Birbal replied, "Jahanpanah, I beg your pardon! But I am late because my wife was not well."

The Emperor said, "Birbal, it seems that you are trying to make an excuse for your late coming . No, I can't believe you."

Birbal was very much surprised to hear the Emperor, as never before he had spoken in such harsh tone to him. Birbal sensed that something was cooking behind him. He smelt that some of his colleagues had poisoned the Emperor's ears. He turned his head to ascertain whose handiwork it could be. Birbal found Sultan Khan's face delighted with exceeding joy. He

at once understood the whole matter. Birbal tried to apologize, but Akbar refused to accept. He then asked, "Your Majesty, should I proceed with administrative work?" Akbar replied, "No!"

Birbal said, "Jahanpanah, please allow me to leave the court and proceed homewards!"

The Emperor answered, "No! You can't."

By that time, Birbal well understood whatever he asked, he would get 'No' as its answer. So he said to the Emperor, "Your Majesty! Please accept my last request. Appoint Sultan Khan's son as your courtier."

The Emperor screamed angrily, "No! Never!"

Sultan Khan was stunned to hear this. Never had he imagined that Birbal would turn the table and shut the future prospects of his son in the court forever. And this time, again clever Birbal beat his opponents with his outstanding wit.

DISTANCING AWAY AN ILL FRIEND

Once, Emperor Akbar was very much worried. The reason was his dear son Salim. The prince was a fine and able boy and was adept in administrative and war skills. However, the prince had a friend named Masoor, who was not so sound in his work and character. Prince Salim's increasing intimacy with his friend was causing him all the harm. He distracted himself from the administrative work and was spending most of his time in pleasure and fun.

Akbar's worry was quite justified. Salim was the heir prince and he had to be very responsible. The Emperor sought advices from a few of his senior courtiers. Some of them suggested the king to have a face-to-face talk with the prince. A few others advised him to apply force and send the prince's friend to some other place. But nothing could appeal to the Emperor, as he knew it very well that all those measures would bring the friend closer to the prince.

At last Akbar turned towards Birbal. Birbal sought a couple of days' time to part the two close friends. On the next day, he called Masoor, the friend of Salim in the court. When he came, the prince was also present there. Birbal called Masoor near him and gave him a seat next to him. He then pretended to whisper something in the ear of Masoor. But in the fact, he did not utter a single word. Birbal repeated it thrice. Masoor was quite puzzled on the strange behaviour of Birbal. Salim too was observing the whole affair sitting at some distance.

The court adjourned and the prince and Masoor came out. Salim was very curious to know what Birbal was telling in the ears of Masoor. He at once approached him and asked, "My dear, what Birbalji was telling in your ears?"

"Nothing, my friend!" replied Masoor.

"What nothing?" retorted the prince, "I saw him whispering something in your ear."

"But he did not say anything. I don't know what he was up to. His behaviour baffled me too," said the friend.

"No Masoor, it seems you don't want to reveal it and thus you are lying. In fact your strange behaviour erokes or doubt in my mind about you," said Salim.

"What! Am I lying? You're doubting my credentials," said the friend angrily.

"Your actions are liable to doubt. I am very much sure that you are hiding something. And now, I don't consider you as my friend," said the prince angrily.

"I too don't want a friend like you, who distrusts the words of his friend!" saying so Masoor went away from there. Prince Salim also moved in another direction breaking their relationship forever.

The Seal

Akbar would often wander alone in disguise to see his administration first hand. However, Birbal had some reservation regarding the Emperor's practice. Birbal viewed that wandering alone, unguarded could be unsafe or even dangerous for the Emperor. He believed that the Emperor's life was invaluable for the country. So he expressed his concern to Akbar several times. But the Emperor took it casually and remained stuck to his old practice.

One day the Emperor disguised himself and ventured out from a secret door to witness his people and their views regarding his administration. When the Emperor was on his way, he felt that he was being

followed. Akbar stopped for a moment and turned back to see the follower. The follower too stopped at some distance and pretended as if he was not interested in him. Akbar began walking ahead. The man also started walking. The Emperor was almost sure that the man was keeping his track. At last, he stopped and asked the man, "What is your name?"

The man replied, "Wan-der-bust!"

"What do you do?" asked Akbar.

"Wandering! It's my favourite profession," replied the stranger.

"Where do you stay?" asked the Emperor. "Everywhere or nowhere!" replied the man quite casually.

Akbar was quite irritated by his puzzling answers.

To bring the man to his right senses, the Emperor

thundered, “Do you know who I am?” The man replied more casually than before, “You are a human being as we all are!”

The Emperor was unable to bear his attitude. So he said, “I’m the Emperor of this state. If you don’t believe, you can see the royal seal.”

The man asked, “Show me your seal.”

Akbar took out the ring to show the man. The seal was embossed on it. The Emperor was desperate to prove himself, so he placed the ring on the stranger’s palm to have a closer look. The man deftly hid the ring in his clothes and started running from there. Before the Emperor could realise his mistake, he has reached some distance away from him. Akbar ran chasing the rogue and shouting for help. The people passing on the way, nabbed him immediately. Before the people could thrash him, he screamed, “You fools, don’t you recognize your Emperor! See the royal seal as the proof.” Saying so, the stranger took out the stolen seal. The people around him at once spared him and apologized heavily for their grave mistake.

The disguised Emperor, who was still at some distance witnessing the whole incident thought, “It’s better I should sneak away from here, or else, I will have to face the ire of these angry people who had wrongly considered the rogue as the Emperor.”

The Emperor rushed back to the palace. On the way, he was very much disturbed on losing his seal. Birbal’s words of caution were resounding in his ears. “Birbal may help me to get the royal seal back,” thought the worried Emperor as a last resort while entering his

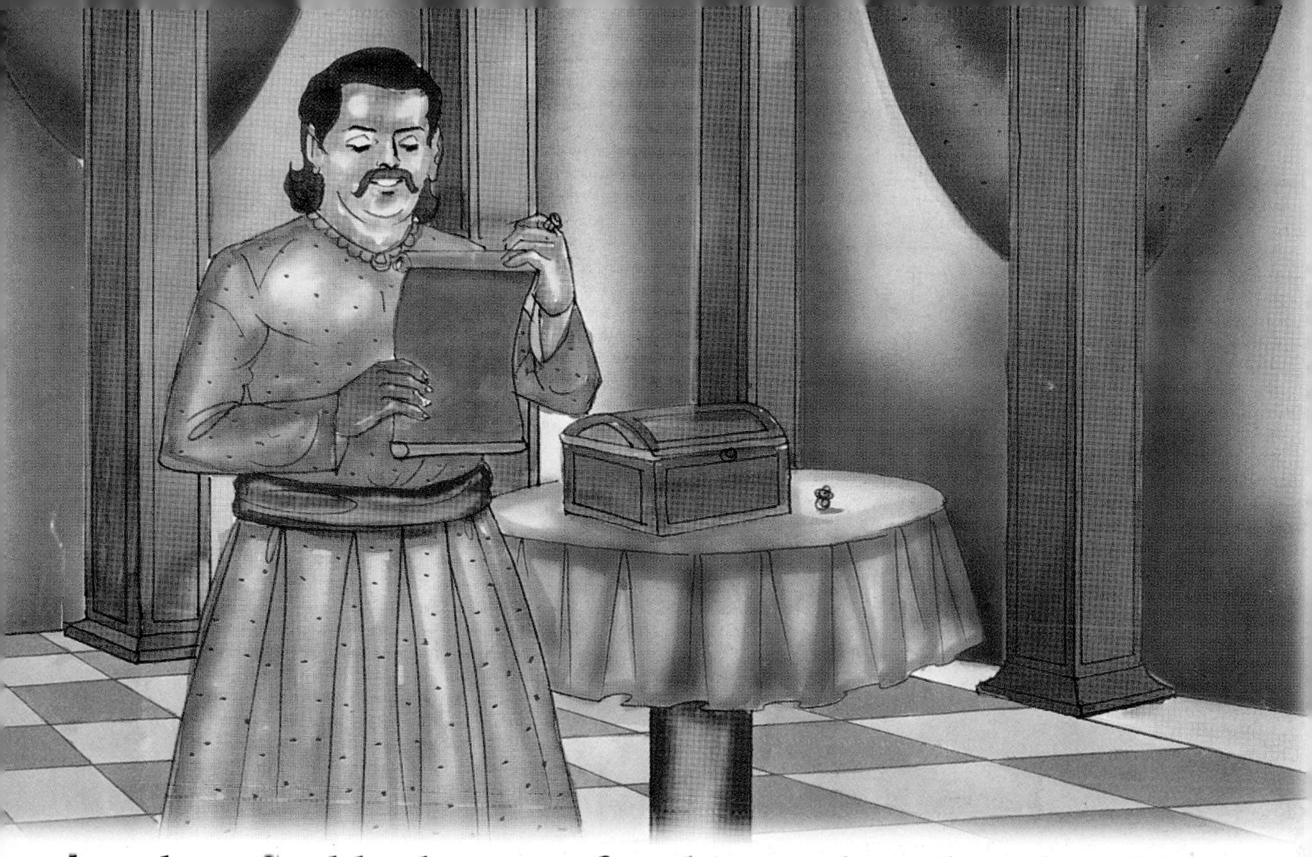

chamber. Suddenly an unfamiliar packet placed on his table fetched his attention. He immediately opened it and found a case inside. He opened the case. Lo and behold! The royal seal was inside the case. A neatly folded paper was placed beside it. Akbar desperately opened it and found a letter written by Birbal.

"Your Majesty, Sorry for the inconvenience. I had warned you against venturing out alone. Today it was the seal, but you could lose any thing. Please take back your seal. Hope you'll understand my compulsion to behave in such strange way."

Akbar heaved a sigh of relief. "Birbal you're great. You taught me a good lesson," thought the Emperor while smiling in his heart.

PALMS WITHOUT HAIR

Birbal had unparalleled wit. It was his intelligence and wit that brought Birbal so close to the Emperor.

One day, Akbar was in a relaxed mood and was

enjoying the company of Birbal. Suddenly the Emperor spread both his palms and asked, "Birbal, can you tell me why there is no hair on my palms".

Birbal gave a pleasing answer, "Jahanpanah, the reason is very simple. Everyday you donate generously to the poor and the needy with both of your hands. How can hair grow on such palms?"

Akbar was pleased with his answer. However he decided to pull Birbal's leg for giving such a pleasing answer. So, he further asked, "If it's so, then why is there no hair on your palms?"

Birbal at once replied, "Jahanpanah, it is also

very simple. Hair of my palms have vanished due to continuous acceptance of gifts and rewards from you."

His clever answers made the Emperor even more eager to outwit Birbal. So he asked again, "Now you must tell me why there is no hair on the hands of other courtiers".

Birbal was too smart to be outwitted. He promptly answered, "Your Majesty, the answer is obvious. Whenever I get rewards from you, the other courtiers rub their hands out of disappointment and envy. The continuous rub does not allow the hair to grow on their palms."

The Most Powerful Weapon

One day, the Emperor asked in the court, "Which is the most powerful weapon?"

A number of courtiers gave a variety of answers. They took the names of different battle weapons. As usual, Birbal had a different answer. He said, "Your Majesty, a man's most powerful weapon is his own intelligence".

Akbar said, "How can you say like this?" Birbal replied, "Your Majesty! First of all, for all these battle weapons, we require intelligence. Without intelligence

these are useless. And the most important fact about this human intelligence is its capacity to save oneself from all the adversities."

Birbal said further, "Your Majesty, a person may lose all his physical weapons but intelligence remains with him forever."

The answer satisfied the Emperor and he applauded Birbal for his knowledge and cleverness.

THE NUMBER OF CROWS

Birbal was the star courtier in the court of Emperor Akbar. Akbar was also very fond of Birbal for

his super intelligence and wit. The other courtiers were always jealous of Birbal. One day, a group of courtiers decided to let Birbal down in front of Akbar.

When everyone, including Birbal was sitting in the court, the senior most courtier appealed to the king, "Your Majesty! You always praise Birbal for his cleverness. If he is so intelligent, then he must tell the court how many crows are present in our kingdom."

Emperor Akbar smiled and looked towards Birbal. Birbal replied instantly, "There are nine thousand nine hundred ninety five crows in our kingdom".

Everyone in the court was astonished to hear his prompt reply.

"Are you sure? If this number doesn't match with the actual number of crows present in the city, then?" asked the Emperor.

Birbal replied coolly, "Your Majesty! My counting is appropriate. If at any time the number of crows is found less, then it will mean that those crows are out

of the city to visit their friends and relatives."

Birbal further said, "And if the number of crows is more than what I have counted, then it will reflect that a few crows from other places have come to visit our city."

"In any case, my counting is absolutely right," Birbal said firmly.

The envious courtiers were at their wit's end. There was no way out to defy his claim. They looked foolishly towards each other.

However, the Emperor laughed aloud to hear his clever reply.

❀ ❀ ❀

Who is Greater

One day, the Emperor and the courtiers were discussing about different mythological gods and their work. One of the courtiers said, "Indra is the king of the heaven and so he is the most powerful among the gods". The other courtiers also agreed with the statement.

Suddenly, the Emperor shot a strange question, "Who is greater, god Indra or I?

Complete silence prevailed in the court. The courtiers looked towards each other. The question was very tricky. If their answer went in the favour of the Emperor, it will not be proper. Besides this, Akbar

will certainly ask the explanation for it. All the eyes turned towards Birbal. Birbal got up and said humbly, "Jahanpanah, there is no doubt that you are greater than god Indra."

The Emperor was not prepared for this answer. Obviously the answer was to please the Emperor. However, he was keen to hear Birbal's explanation. So he said, "Birbal, now you must justify your statement".

Birbal replied, "Your Majesty, when lord Brahma created this universe, he made two worlds - heaven and the earth. The residents of heaven were gods and

the residents of the earth were human beings. To rule the worlds, he created two icons. One was of Indra and the other was of yours Jahanpanah!"

The whole court was peacefully hearing Birbal's explanation.

Birbal continued, "After creating two wonderful images, Lord had to decide where to send each of them? So lord placed the images on either side of the balance. Soon the tray of the balance carrying your image started going down. And finally it reached the earth. As your image was heavier than god Indra, Lord Brahma decided to give you the kingdom of the earth and made Indra the king of heaven."

Akbar laughed heartily on Birbal's pleasing but clever reply.

A Cock Amidst Hens

After years of interaction, the Emperor realised that it was not an easy job to outwit Birbal. Despite this, he sometimes tried to do so.

One day, when Birbal was yet to reach the court, Akbar carefully chalked out a plan in connivance with the other courtiers to embarrass him. The Emperor distributed one egg of hen each to all the courtiers

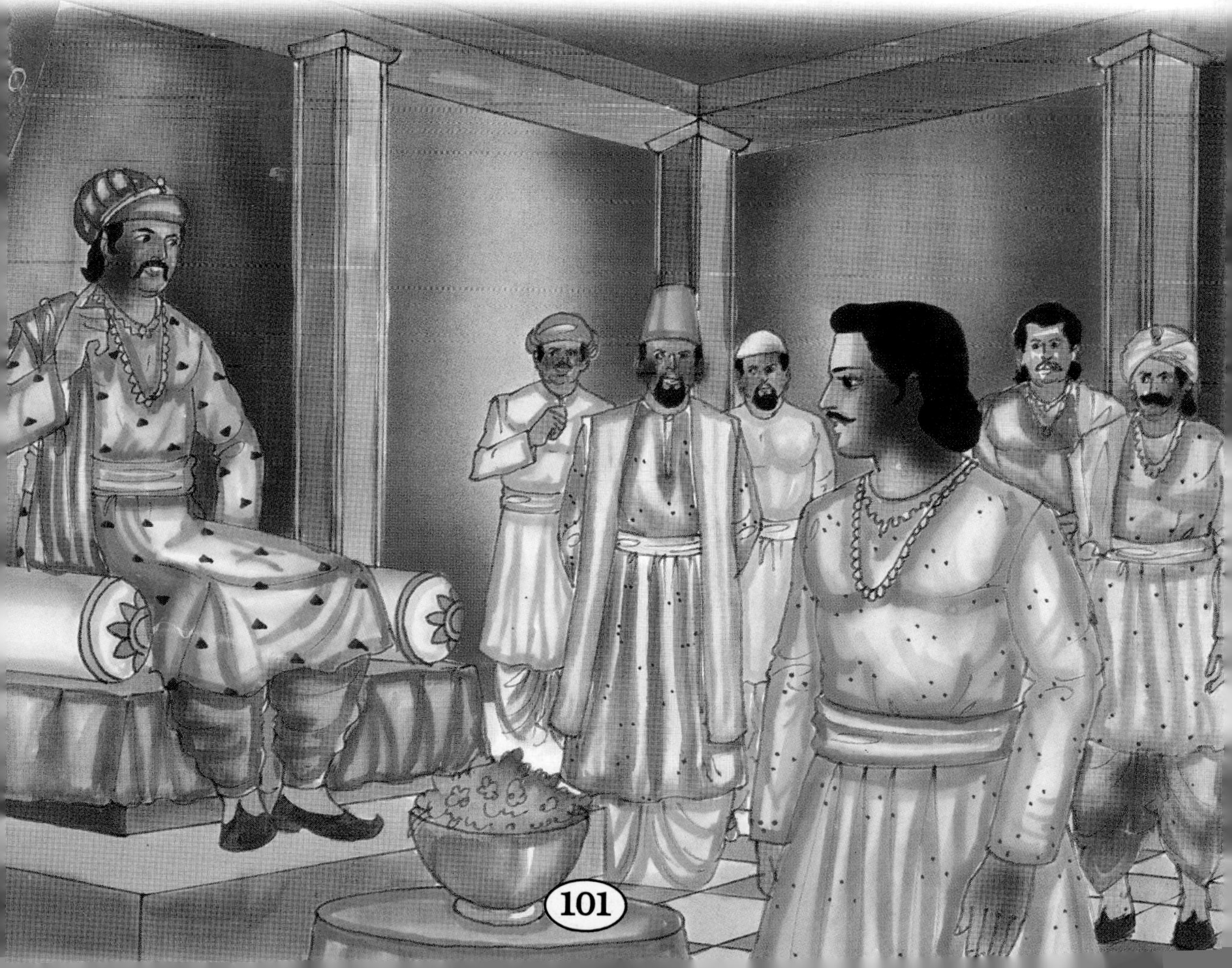

and asked them to hide the eggs in their clothes.

When Birbal came to the court, the Emperor announced, "Last night I had a peculiar dream. In my dream, a sage suggested to me to test the loyalty of my courtiers. He advised me to ask the courtiers to take a dip into the royal pool. All the courtiers, who come out with an egg after taking a dip are loyal to me and the rest are not. Now, I want to test the loyalty of all my courtiers."

With this, Akbar directed all his courtiers to proceed towards the royal pool. Everyone rushed to the pool. There, each one took a dip and came out with an egg in hand. Finally it was Birbal's turn to jump into the pool. He dipped into the pool and tried hard

to find the hen's egg, but he could not. He immediately understood whose plot it could be to tease him.

Birbal came out of the water and started crowing like a cock, "Cock-a-doodle-do! Cock-a-doodle-do!...."

Irritated by the repeated crowing, the Emperor shouted, "Stop behaving foolishly, Birbal! Where is your egg?"

"Sorry Your Majesty! After dipping into the water I realised that I was a cock unlike these hens and so I could not lay eggs," replied Birbal.

The courtiers looked at each other foolishly with eggs in their hands.

Once again their attempt to tease the wise Birbal failed.

❀ ❀ ❀

THE SHORT STICK

It was a proven fact that Birbal was exceptionally intelligent. He was always ready with his prompt answer for each and every question, irrespective of how difficult or peculiar that was.

One day, the Emperor and Birbal were strolling in the garden. Suddenly Akbar picked up a piece of bamboo stick lying on the ground. Just to outwit Birbal, he asked, "Can you make this stick short without cutting it?"

Birbal thought for a while. Then he picked up

another bamboo stick lying on the ground. It was longer than the stick, which the Emperor was holding in his hand. He gave this stick to Akbar and said, "Jahanpanah! Now look at the first stick. Without cutting, it's looking smaller."

The emperor did not say anything. He smiled and looked at Birbal with praise.

PANDITJI

In the city of Delhi, there lived a Brahmin. The Brahmin loved to eat and sleep. He was fat and lazy. During his childhood, he was never inclined towards his studies. So, he could not acquire the knowledge of the Vedas and Shastras. He had a desire that people should call him 'Panditji'. Whenever he saw any learned person being called as 'Panditji', his desire would further get strengthened. But how could it be possible? The person who did not know the ABCs of the Vedas

and Shastras could not be called so respectfully.

So much intense was his desire that one day the Brahmin went to Birbal. He said, "Maharaj! You are the wisest of wise. I've come to you with a big hope." The Brahmin continued, "I'm not a learned person. Nevertheless, I crave that people should call me 'Panditji'."

"But how come it's possible? Before aspiring for this, you must acquire proper knowledge," replied Birbal.

"No sir, it's not possible for me. I've come to you with a great hope. Please do something so that the people will start calling me 'Panditji'. That's good enough for me," said the Brahmin in very desperate voice. Birbal thought for a while, then he asked the Brahmin to pass by his house the next morning.

Next day early in the morning, the Brahmin went towards Birbal's house and started walking by the house. Birbal, who was waiting there for the Brahmin, called a few street children who were playing in the lane. He whispered in their ears, "If you call this fat man 'Panditji', he will get irritated".

For those amusement-loving children, it was a good opportunity to make fun. So they all started shouting together, "Panditji! Panditji! Panditji...!" while walking behind the Brahmin. The children continued to call him amidst their giggle.

The whole matter made the Brahmin very irritated. He tried to stop the children from calling him like this. But the children did not stop. Unable to control his anger, the Brahmin picked up stones and started throwing them towards the children. However, it further aggravated the matter. The children swiftly ran to a safe distance and started calling him 'Panditji', even louder than before.

The scene attracted other passersby and soon they recognized the Brahmin as Panditji.

This continued for a few more days. Slowly and slowly more people knew the Brahmin by his new name 'Panditji'. The Brahmin's long cherished wish was fulfilled. But then, he was not a happy man. The word 'Panditji' used for him sounded funny and irritating to him. However what could he do now?

❀ ❀ ❀

THE OIL SELLER AND THE BUTCHER

Once, two persons, an oil seller and a butcher appeared in front of Birbal with their dispute.

When Birbal enquired about the dispute, the butcher said, "Sir, this man came to buy mutton from my shop. When I turned to cut the mutton, he picked up my bag of coins from the counter. When I tried to stop him, he claimed that it belonged to him."

The oil seller interrupted, "Your Majesty, this man is lying. I went to buy mutton from his shop. After buying mutton I took out my bag to pay him. Seeing the bag full of money, the butcher all of a sudden started shouting that I had picked up his money. Now only you can render justice to me."

Birbal asked both the parties to divulge the truth. However, both of them remained adamant on their respective statements.

At last Birbal called his servant and asked him to bring a vessel filled with water. He then emptied the bag into the water.

Birbal carefully examined the water. He found that the colour of the water had started changing. Soon the water took pink colour. The change in colour indicated that the money belonged to the butcher. Actually, the coins in the bag were received with blood stained hands. And so the coins were also stained with blood.

Birbal gave the money to the butcher and fined the oil seller for troubling the butcher and misleading the court.

The Donkey's Load

One day, the Emperor and the Empress went to take bath in the river Yamuna. Akbar's favourite companion Birbal also accompanied them.

Before entering into the water, the royal couple entrusted the responsibility of taking care of their clothes and ornaments to Birbal.

The Emperor and the Empress then entered into the river to enjoy the cool water, while Birbal remained out looking after their belongings.

The Emperor was totally relaxed and was in a mood of fun. He looked at Birbal, who was standing on the bank and doing quite an odd job. The Emperor whispered in Empress' ear, "Birbal is looking quite foolish guarding our clothes. Just watch how I tease him."

Akbar then shouted from the middle of the river, "Birbal! You are looking like standing with a donkey's load."

Birbal was smart enough.

He promptly replied, "You are absolutely right Your Majesty! My condition is really pathetic. I'm standing here not with one donkey's load but with the load of two donkeys."

❀ ❀ ❀

THE EMPEROR ATE THE FOOD OF HORSE

One day, the Emperor and Birbal went for hunting with the royal cavalcade. While chasing the prey, they reached into the deep forest.

By the time they could realize that they were far away from the city, it was quite late. Evening was

setting in and they had nothing to eat and drink.

The Emperor was feeling very hungry. Both of them sat on a tree and waited for the royal cavalcade to come. After sometime, when the Emperor could not tolerate his hunger any more, he said to Birbal, "I'm feeling very hungry. Is there something to eat?"

Birbal thought for a while, then climbed down and brought a bag of roasted gram, which was tied on the neck of his horse. It was horse's food.

As there was no other option, the Emperor started chewing the roasted gram. Since he was very hungry, he finished the entire bag.

After taking rest for sometime, they decided to move from there. When Birbal tried to mount upon his horse's back, the horse neighed vigorously. Surprised by this unusual behaviour, the Emperor asked, "Why did the horse neigh like this?"

"Your Majesty! The horse saw you eating his food. Now he is asking me on whom I'm going to ride? On him or on you?" replied Birbal gently.

The Emperor remained silent for a moment and then laughed aloud on his joke.

❀ ❀ ❀

THE MAGICAL STICK

In the city of Delhi, there lived a rich merchant. He always wore a thick diamond studded necklace. One day before going for a bath, he removed his necklace and hung it in his bedroom. After taking bath when he came back, he found the necklace missing. The merchant searched the necklace everywhere. But he could not find it out. At last, he called all his five servants and enquired with them about the missing necklace. However, all of them refused to accept the crime.

It was certain that one of the servants had stolen the necklace. But it was not easy to identify the thief

among them. So, the merchant decided to go to the court of the Emperor.

Akbar heard the case and asked Birbal to investigate it. Birbal called all the servants, gave one stick to each of them and said, "These sticks are no ordinary sticks. These are magical ones. Till tomorrow, the stick of the thief will grow by two inches. Then it will be very easy to identify the thief with his longer stick." With this, Birbal sent all the servants back to their place and instructed them to appear in the court the next day with their respective sticks.

That night when all were sleeping, the thief among the servants was restless.

"This magical stick will grow tomorrow and I'll certainly be caught and punished. I must do something to save myself," thought the servant, who had stolen the chain.

After thinking for sometime, he cut two inches from his stick and made it shorter. Then the guilty servant slept peacefully. He was happy and satisfied with his arrangement.

Next day, the merchant appeared in the court with all his servants. Birbal asked the servants to produce their sticks.

One by one, all the servants presented Birbal with their sticks. Birbal observed all the sticks very carefully. When the servant who had stolen the necklace gave his stick to Birbal, the wise man

immediately said, "Your Majesty! He is the thief among these servants."

"But my stick is not longer than the other sticks. It's shorter!" the servant tried to argue.

"You fool! There is no magic in these sticks", remarked Birbal, "I knew that the thief would certainly try to make it shorter considering it a magical stick and you did the same."

The scared servant fell on Birbal's feet and accepted his crime. He returned the necklace to the merchant.

The merchant gratefully thanked Birbal and went away.

THE RIGHT TEST

Once the royal army required new shields for the soldiers. So the Emperor asked the minister in charge of defense to give the contract of shields to any good shield making company.

There were many contenders for this big contract. One of them was an excellent producer of shields and most of the royal shields had been bought from his company. The shields manufactured by the company were indeed of very good quality.

The minister in the charge of defense was a dishonest man. He wanted to get commission from the shield contractor. But the contractor refused to pay any commission as his work was excellent.

On the predetermined day, the contractor appeared in the court with his shield for its evaluation. As the defense minister wanted to lay the contractor down, so he suggested the Emperor to test the shield by putting it under elephant's foot.

Since the shield was not designed to withstand so much of weight, it cracked under elephant's weight. The Emperor became angry and refused to give the contract to him.

The contractor was very much disappointed and sad. He went to meet Birbal, who was not present in the court that day.

The contractor told Birbal everything about the unusual test and the motive of the dishonest minister.

Birbal asked the contractor to come on the next day with another such shield and assured him of justice.

Next day the contractor appeared in the court with a new shield. The Emperor got annoyed to see the contractor. He asked, “I've already refused to give the contract to you. Then why have you come here again?”

Birbal answered on behalf of the contractor, "Your Majesty, shields are made for protecting the soldiers from the attack of sword. It's not supposed to tolerate the heavy load and pressure. So I request you to test the shield for its utility."

The Emperor found sense in Birbal's words. He at once called two soldiers with swords. First soldier attacked with the sword on the shield, which the other soldier was holding in his hand. After a long testing, the soldiers concluded that the shield was tough enough and it fitted into their requirement.

The Emperor was also satisfied. So he awarded the contract on the same contractor.

The contractor expressed his gratitude to Birbal for speaking on his behalf and went away happily.